Special thanks to:

Irene Bofill, for creating all the beautiful illustrations in the book. Your patience and meticulous attention to detail were so appreciated.

Michael Lund, for providing all the fabulous bird photographs used throughout the book.

The talented students in Ms. Perilman's 2018-2019 fourth grade class at Granby Elementary in Worthington, Ohio, who helped edit the manuscript.

My friends at Rookery Bay, who provided me with great insights into the flora and fauna throughout the preserve—Sarah Falkowski, Anne Mauro, and Jared Franklin.

Melissa Falter—the punctuation and grammar queen!

And of course my loving family, Maury, Garrett, and Ellie, who never tired of reading draft after draft.

www.mascotbooks.com

JENNY'S FIRST CATCH

For more information, please contact:
Mascot Books
620 Herndon Parkway, Suite 320
Herndon, VA 20170
info@mascotbooks.com

Library of Congress Control Number: 2020907626

CPSIA Code: PRTWP0620A
ISBN-13: 978-1-64543-560-0

Printed in Malaysia

Enjoy learning about Jenny and all her feathered friends. Keep an eye out for them as you explore beautiful Florida!

Susan Levine

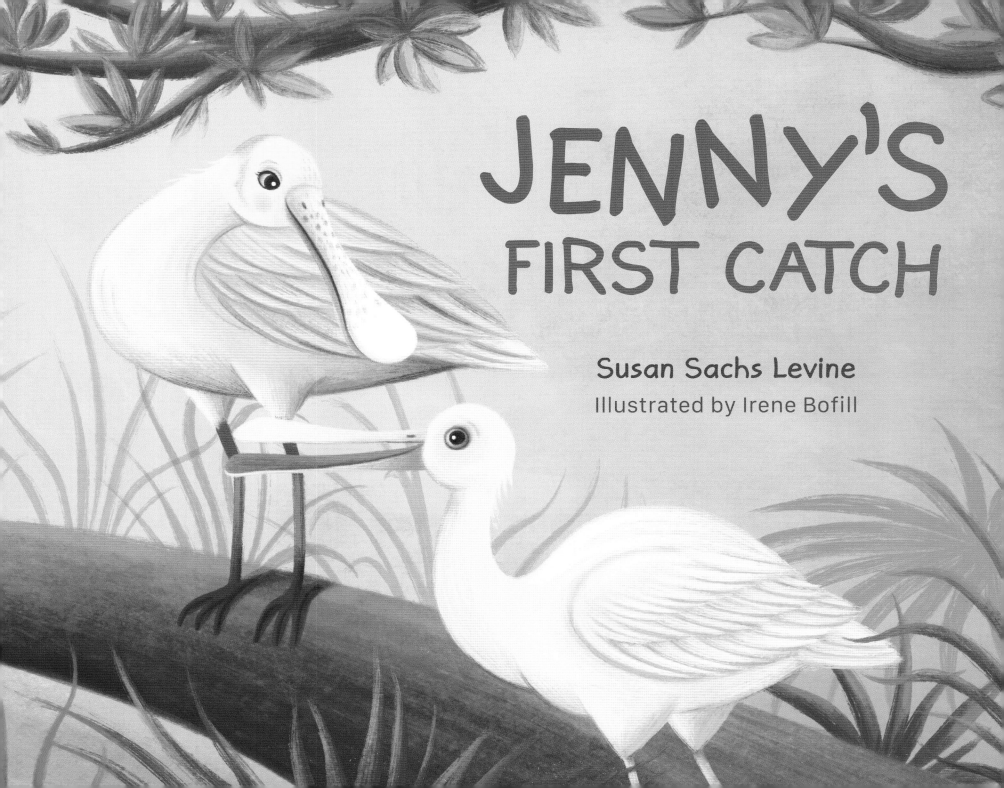

JENNY'S
FIRST CATCH

Susan Sachs Levine

Illustrated by Irene Bofill

WHY JENNY AND MAY?

I chose the names Jenny and May for the Roseate Spoonbill chicks in honor of May Mann Jennings, who served as first lady of Florida while her husband, William Sherman Jennings, was governor from 1901-1905. She was a recognized leader in conservation and an outspoken critic of plume hunting. She helped protect the Everglades and create the Everglades National Park.

"Stay here, Jenny, while I check on your sister back at the nest. Then I'll teach you how to fish. You're so grown up!" exclaimed Jenny's mother.

Welcome to
Rookery Bay
Reserve

Jenny felt proud that she had fledged the nest first, before her sister, May. As she wandered along the water's edge, she noticed several birds feeding.

It can't be that hard to catch a little fish, Jenny thought. *I'll teach myself and surprise Mom. I'm sure I can do it!*

"Excuse me Miss Yellow Feet, can you teach me how to fish? I'm going to surprise my mom," explained Jenny, politely.

"Oh, I love surprises," replied the Snowy Egret, enthusiastically. "It's simple. First, grasp a branch over the water. Second, stretch your neck until you can see the fish. Third, be very still, and when a tasty one swims near, snap it up in your beak."

The Snowy thrust her head forward like a flash of lightning and came up with a wiggling little fish that she flipped up and swallowed whole.

"Awesome! My turn," said Jenny. She stepped carefully onto a branch and spied several fish. She quickly plunged her bill down into the water, but all that happened was a big SPLASH that scared the fish away.

"Great try, but that bill of yours is a bit too big for fishing," said the Snowy.

SNOWY EGRET

The Snowy Egret is one of the most elegant herons, with a slender, all-white body, black bill, long black legs, and brilliant yellow feet. During the breeding season, adults **molt** and develop long wispy feathers on their back, neck, and head that were prized by **plume hunters** to decorate women's hats in the late 1800s. With plumes once valued at twice the price of gold per ounce, Snowy Egrets were hunted to near extinction.

Snowy Egrets live along the coast and prefer shallow water habitats. They can be seen standing still or shuffling their yellow feet in the water to attract aquatic animals including fish, frogs, worms, and crustaceans.

The Snowy Egret nests in trees, shrubs, and mangroves in mixed colonies of wading birds. When one mate takes over on the nest for the other, it will often present a stick, as if passing a baton. **Immature** Snowy Egrets look similar to adults but have duller, greenish legs.

Just then, a flock of white birds with long curved bills fluttered in for a landing.

"Excuse me Curvy Billed Birds, can you please teach me how you catch fish?" asked Jenny.

"Fish are not our favorite. We prefer crabs, worms, snails, and insects–chewy and delicious," announced the closest White Ibis. Then they all started poking their sharp bills into the mud and pulling up critters that they slurped down.

"Give it a try, little lady. You barely have to get your feet wet," encouraged a second Ibis.

Stab, stab, stab went Jenny's bill, but all her head felt was BAM, BAM, BAM! A little dizzy, she staggered away.

"Nice try, but I think your bill needs to be pointed like ours," remarked one of the Ibises.

Fishing is harder than it looks, but as Mom always says, 'If at first you don't succeed, try, try again,' thought Jenny.

WHITE IBIS

The White Ibis is a gregarious wading bird that feeds and roosts in large groups. It is distinguished by a curved, reddish-pink bill, long red legs, and a white body. The White Ibis has black wingtips that are visible in flight.

A White Ibis habitat is any type of shallow water—marshes, mudflats, or mangrove **estuaries**. Ibises feed by probing with their bills to feel for prey. They can also **forage** in mud or short grass. Their favorite diet is crayfish and crabs.

The White Ibis nests in mixed colonies in mangroves or tree thickets. When the young hatch, their bills are straight and don't start to curve downward until they are 14 days old. The **immature** birds are a patchwork of white and brown with a pink bill and pink legs.

BROWN PELICAN

The Brown Pelican is a large, stocky seabird with a long neck and a giant bill. The adults have gray-brown bodies with white necks and yellow heads. During the breeding season, the neck has a dark reddish-brown stripe. **Immature** birds are gray-brown all over.

Brown Pelicans are found in flocks, often gliding in a V or single-file line low across coastal waters. Despite their size, an average Brown Pelican weighs only 7-8 pounds.

The Brown Pelican lives along seacoasts, saltwater bays, and mangrove **estuaries.** They feed primarily on fish by rising up to 60 feet above the water and then plunging down headfirst. The impact stuns small fish that the pelicans scoop up with their big bills.

The Brown Pelican nests in colonies, and the parents take turns incubating the eggs under their huge webbed feet. The chicks fledge the nest after about 90 days, but the parents continue to care for them for 8-10 months.

A big KER–SPLASH startled Jenny. She saw a huge bird with a bill like a bucket pop up in the water. He tipped his head down so that water drained out and all he had left was a mouthful of tasty little fish.

"A whole buffet!" shouted Jenny. "Hey Mr. Bucket Bird, can you teach me to do that?"

"Can you fly up high?" asked the Brown Pelican.

"Yes sir, I've been flying for three days," replied Jenny, confidently.

"Let's go!" the Pelican called as he lifted into the air. "When you see a school of fish, dive straight down. Then open your bill and scoop them up."

He splashed down with Jenny close behind. COUGH, CHOKE, SPUTTER. Instead of fish, Jenny just came up with a mouthful of water.

"Good go, but that bill of yours is just not big enough for this type of fishing," said the Pelican, sympathetically.

"What?" cried a frustrated Jenny. "First my bill is too big and now my bill is too small!"

AMERICAN ALLIGATOR

The American Alligator is the largest reptile in the U.S. and can reach lengths of 12 feet and weigh as much as 1,000 pounds! It has an armored-looking body, a long muscular tail, and powerful jaws with 80 sharp teeth. Alligators are the closest relatives to dinosaurs of all living reptiles.

The American Alligator is cold-blooded, meaning it gets its body heat from the environment. It can often be seen sunning itself along the banks of rivers, lakes, and swamps. Alligators are carnivores, hunting fish, frogs, wading birds, snakes, and small mammals, primarily at night.

Female alligators lay 20-60 eggs in big nest mounds near the shore. The hatchlings are just 6-8 inches long with yellow and black stripes. The mother protects and cares for them for up to 2 years.

American Alligators were nearly hunted to extinction due to demand for their hides for purses, shoes, and belts. Today they are common in Florida, but still vulnerable to **habitat loss.**

As a disheartened Jenny continued on, she felt her stomach rumble. *Catching food is taking longer than I thought. I'll bet Mom is getting worried. I should head back. But which way is home?!*

Suddenly she had the feeling that two eyes were following her. *Oh no, now I'm hungry, lost, and about to be someone else's dinner!*

"Mom, where are you?" shouted a panicked Jenny as she flew up and away from the alligator's snapping jaws.

"What's wrong, sad little bird?" asked a Wood Stork. Looking up, Jenny saw two birds with heads that looked like tree bark.

"I'm so hungry and I'm trying to learn how to fish, but my bill is not working and now I'm lost!" exclaimed an upset Jenny.

"If you want to fish, watch me," offered the kindly Wood Stork. "Just stand on one leg, then open your bill and place it down in the water. Dig in the mud with your other foot, and when a crab or crayfish swims out, snap your bill closed!"

Jenny lifted one leg. Teetering, tottering...PLOP! She fell over. She tried again, slowly...carefully...CRASH!

"I'm so clumsy," she groaned.

"Chin up! It just takes a little practice," offered the Wood Stork.

WOOD STORK

The Wood Stork is a hefty wading bird with long legs and a thick bill. Standing over 3 feet tall, Wood Storks are entirely white except for black flight feathers and a black tail. The head is un-feathered and dark in color.

The Wood Stork inhabits swamps and wetlands. It **forages** by wading in shallow water with its head down and bill partially open. It digs in the muddy bottom with one foot to scare up prey and then quickly snaps its bill shut. A Wood Stork's diet is mostly fish, but crayfish, crabs, frogs, and small reptiles are also on the menu.

Nesting occurs in colonies of several hundred Wood Storks in mangrove or cypress forests. Wood Stork parents have been seen spitting up water onto the nestlings to keep them cool. **Immature** Wood Storks resemble the adults except for a feathered head and a yellow bill. Wood Stork populations have decreased significantly due to **habitat loss**.

Tired, muddy, and bruised, Jenny forged ahead. A majestic and wise-looking bird stood at the edge of the mangroves. *I'll try fishing one more time,* she thought. *I can't give up!*

"Excuse me Mrs. Wise Bird, how come I'm not catching any food when all the other birds seem to be hauling in plenty?" inquired Jenny with a sigh.

"We are all wading birds...but with different bodies, different bills, and different diets. You have to be yourself. Don't try to catch food like the others," explained the Great Blue Heron. "I have a big, pointed bill. I catch fish by being very still and then springing my neck forward to snatch them out of the water. Other shore birds eat crabs, crayfish, and frogs down in the mud, so they need to poke and prod with their bill or foot."

"Like the birds with the curvy orange bills that I met!" exclaimed Jenny.

"Exactly," said the Heron. "You are a Roseate Spoonbill with a very special bill. I've seen Spoonbills catch all kinds of fish, crabs, and tasty critters."

"REALLY?" cried Jenny.

"I see some Roseate Spoonbills in the next cove," observed the Great Blue Heron.

GREAT BLUE HERON

The Great Blue Heron is a very large, majestic wading bird with subtle blue-gray feathers. Its head features a long, thick, orange-yellowish bill and a thin, black plume that extends out over its neck. Despite a height of over 4 feet, the Great Blue Heron weighs only 5-6 pounds due to its hollow bones. In flight, it looks enormous with a wingspan of 6 feet.

The Great Blue Heron thrives around all kinds of water, including salt or fresh.

A hunting Great Blue Heron will wade slowly or stand statue-like, stalking fish and other prey in shallow water. Specially shaped neck bones allow for a lightning-fast thrust of the head as they stab fish, shrimp, crabs, frogs, turtles, or snakes with their strong bills.

Breeding Great Blue Herons gather in colonies of up to 500 birds and build bulky stick nests high off the ground. **Immature** birds are duller in color than the adults and lack the head plume.

"Are you Jenny?" inquired a beautiful pink bird. "I'm Marjory. Your mom was just here in a panic looking for you."

"Yes, I'm Jenny. I was trying to surprise her and teach myself to fish, but I haven't had any success yet, and now I'm hungry and lost!"

"Let me help. My daughter, Daisy, can go find your mom while I give you a quick lesson on catching critters with a spoonbill," suggested Marjory.

"One, two, three, and off I go,
Be right back with Jenny's mom in tow!"
rhymed Daisy as she skipped away.

ROSEATE SPOONBILL

The Roseate Spoonbill is a shy, medium-sized water bird. It is beautiful from a distance with pale-pink feathers and bright pink shoulders and rump. Up close, it looks bizarre with red eyes, a bald yellowish-green head, and a giant spoon-shaped bill.

Roseate Spoonbills are found in coastal marshes, mudflats, and mangrove **estuaries**. They **forage** in shallow water by slowly sweeping their partly opened bill from side to side feeling for crustaceans such as shrimp and crabs, aquatic insects, and fish. The prey tickles the fine hairs inside their bill, causing it to snap shut! The Roseate Spoonbill gets its pink color from the crustaceans it eats.

Roseate Spoonbills nest in trees in mixed colonies. The **juveniles** look similar to adults but are paler pink and have feathered heads. When the chicks hatch, their bills are flat and become spoon-shaped as they grow.

Spoonbills were nearly eliminated in the 1860s due to **plume hunting.** They are still uncommon and vulnerable to human disturbance.

Smiling at Daisy's antics, Marjory continued, "Obviously spoonbills are not good for stabbing and poking, so we can't fish like some of the other birds."

"You got that right," agreed Jenny, thinking of all her unsuccessful attempts.

"A spoonbill is special–it is uniquely adapted for sweeping from side to side and finding little fish, crab, shrimp, and insects," continued Marjory.

Jenny watched Marjory sweep her bill back and forth and quickly come up with a little crab.

"BRAVO!" Jenny cheered.

Jenny placed her bill into the water.
SWEEP, SWEEP, SWEEP.
She went from side to side through the mud,
but the water got cloudy.

"I can't see the fish, Marjory!" exclaimed Jenny.
"That's okay. You are trying to FEEL the fish
with the edge of your bill. Wait until you feel a
tickle," said Marjory.

Jenny placed her bill back down into the water and
waited, and waited, and waited...

"I feel something!" she blurted out as she popped
up. "But I didn't catch it."

"Not yet," encouraged a patient Marjory. "Now this
time, keep your bill slightly open, so when you feel a
tickle you can snap it shut."

With determination, Jenny slowly started sweeping. Nothing, nothing, nothing, until finally...

"GOT IT! My spoonbill *does* work!"

"Terrific! Now quick, hide! Here comes your mom," directed Marjory.

"What's this all about, Daisy? I don't have time for riddles when I can't find my daughter," exclaimed Jenny's mom.

"Answer this and you'll be on your way," replied Daisy.

"Who is super sweet and kind,
turning more beautiful pink with time?
She has a bill like a spoon,
which she wields in the bay beyond the dune.
She catches critters—yes, so many.
The name she goes by rhymes with penny."

"It sounds like Jenny, but..."

Surprise!

"SURPRISE!" yelled Jenny as she jumped out from behind the reeds and proudly dropped a pinfish at her mother's feet.

"Oh, Jenny! I'm so happy to see you. HOW did you catch that?!" said Jenny's mother.

"Fishing isn't so hard," began Jenny. "You just have to keep trying and be true to yourself. We are the only wading birds with a spoonbill—perfect for sweeping the muddy bottom and finding little crabs, fish, and insects that other birds can't catch with their pointed bills."

"You sure learned a lot in one morning," observed Jenny's mom.

"I had a little help from some friends," Jenny said with a smile.

"How about we put all that knowledge to good use and let you teach your sister to fish? She fledged this morning!" announced Jenny's mom, stepping aside to reveal May.

Jenny stopped abruptly and beamed at her mother and sister. "I sure will!" she said.

"Come on, May, the first thing you need to know is that you have a **very special spoonbill**," said Jenny as she proudly led the way.

GLOSSARY OF TERMS

ESTUARY: A body of water formed where a river meets the sea. The water is brackish, meaning it is a mixture of fresh and salt water. Estuaries serve as a natural filter for water that runs off land and are a vital nursery ground for young fish, shrimp, crabs, and other marine creatures. Wading birds rely on estuaries for food and a place to breed.

FLEDGE: When a young bird develops flight feathers that allow it to leave the nest. For wading birds this is generally 6-8 weeks from hatching.

FORAGE: To gather food for immediate consumption or future storage. Wading birds forage in different ways depending on their diet and bill size and shape.

HABITAT LOSS: When an ecosystem is so dramatically changed that it can no longer support its native wildlife. Agriculture, logging, oil and gas exploration, filling in wetlands, and building dams are just a few of the ways that habitats are destroyed. Habitat loss is the number one threat to the survival of wildlife in the United States.

IMMATURE/JUVENILE: Immature refers to a bird that is not yet an adult. Juvenile is more specific and describes a young bird that still has its juvenile plumage. While song birds might have juvenile plumage for just a few weeks, wading birds can have this plumage for up to a year.

MOLT: The replacement of all or some of the feathers on a bird. Young birds molt so they can acquire their adult plumage. Adult birds molt to replace worn or damaged feathers so they are in top flying condition. Adults also molt in the spring to have a new look during the breeding season.

PLUMAGE: The layer of feathers that cover a bird's body. Plumage can also refer to the pattern, colors, and arrangement of the feathers. Plumage varies greatly between species and can indicate the age and sex of the bird, as well as the season.

PLUME HUNTING: The hunting of birds to harvest their feathers for decorative purposes, such as adorning women's hats. This was so common in the late 1800s that the Snowy Egret and other wading birds were nearly extinct in Florida by the turn of the century.

BEST PLACES TO OBSERVE WADING BIRDS IN SOUTHWEST FLORIDA

Generally, wading birds are best viewed at low tide when prey is easier to reach. Winter months are good times as well, when the migratory birds are in Florida and water levels in the swamps are receding, so prey is more concentrated. All of these destinations offer a variety of naturalist-led walks, boat trips, and other programs that I would encourage you to take advantage of by checking out their websites.

BIG CYPRESS NATIONAL PRESERVE
www.nps.gov/bicy/index.htm

BIRD ROOKERY SWAMP
https://crewtrust.org/bird-rookery-swamp-trail/

CORKSCREW SWAMP SANCTUARY
www.corkscrew.audubon.org

EAGLE LAKES COMMUNITY PARK
www.colliercountyfl.gov

J.N. DING DARLING NATIONAL WILDLIFE REFUGE
www.fws.gov/refuge/jn_ding_darling

LAKE TRAFFORD
www.airboatsandalligators.com

ROOKERY BAY RESEARCH RESERVE
www.rookerybay.org

SHARK VALLEY
www.sharkvalleytramtours.com

SIX MILE CYPRESS SLOUGH
www.sloughpreserve.org/preserve

TEN THOUSAND ISLANDS NATIONAL WILDLIFE REFUGE
www.fws.gov/refuge/Ten_Thousand_Islands

TIGERTAIL BEACH
www.tigertailbeach.net

SOME OF THE LAWS THAT PROTECT WADING BIRDS

ENDANGERED SPECIES ACT (ESA): A U.S. federal law that protects endangered and threatened species throughout their range and the ecosystems they rely on for survival. The United States Fish and Wildlife Service determines which species are in need of protection under the ESA.

FLORIDA ENDANGERED AND THREATENED SPECIES ACT: A Florida state law that provides for research and management to conserve and protect threatened and endangered species as a natural resource. The Florida Fish and Wildlife Conservation Commission directs these efforts.

MIGRATORY BIRD TREATY ACT (MBTA): A multi-national agreement between the United States, Great Britain, Canada, Mexico, Japan, and Russia that protects migratory birds which move between the nations. Currently more than 1,000 species are protected.

MORE WADING BIRDS YOU MAY ENCOUNTER

Hey junior birders, can you find these additional seven wading birds hidden in the story? Look carefully at all the illustrations and see how many you can find. Good luck!

BLACK-CROWNED NIGHT HERON: Small, stocky heron that often sits with its head tucked in, creating a hunchback appearance. Adults have a distinctive black cap and back that contrasts with its whitish belly. It generally forages alone after dusk and uses its thick bill to grab fish, insects, lizards, clams, and other marine animals at the water's edge.

GREEN HERON: Small, stocky heron with a dagger-like bill. Plumage is deep green with a chestnut neck and breast. Often sits alone with its neck tucked in on a branch near the water and waits patiently for fish or amphibians to come within striking distance. May raise its head feathers into a crest when taking flight.

LITTLE BLUE HERON: Small heron with slate-blue feathers and a subtle maroon neck and head. Their dull colors and lack of showy plumes spared them during the plume-hunting era. The young are all-white and can easily be mistaken for a Snowy Egret, except the Little Blue Heron has dull green legs and feet. They are patient predators and will stand and wait in shallow water for prey to come close.

GREAT EGRET: Tall, long-legged wading bird with an S-curved neck and a long, dagger-like bill. All feathers on Great Egrets are white. During breeding season, elegant plumes grow from its back and are used in courtship displays. They hunt for fish, frogs, and other aquatic animals by standing still and then quickly striking with their sharp bill.

REDDISH EGRET: Medium to large egret with a shaggy rust-colored neck, a slate-gray body, and a heavy bill. An active feeder, the Reddish Egret may run through the shallows, leap in the air, or raise up both wings as it stabs at fish.

YELLOW-CROWNED NIGHT HERON: A stocky, compact heron with a boldly marked black-and-white head and a yellow crown. They often hunt at night by perching on stumps or branches that hang out over the water. Their prey is primarily crustaceans, including crabs and crayfish.

TRI-COLOR OR LOUISIANA HERON: A medium-sized, delicate-looking heron with a long, pointed bill. Plumage is blue-grey or lavender with a distinctive white underside. It often wades out to belly-deep water where it can stab fish, frogs, and insects.

HABITAT PARTITIONING

Habitat partitioning is when similar species use the same ecosystem in different ways so that they are not directly competing and can all live together successfully. Wading birds are uniquely adapted to catch and eat different organisms based on the size and shape of their bills and their dietary needs.

For example, Snowy Egrets and Little Blue Herons have medium-sized, pointed bills and eat fish near the surface. A Great Egret or Great Blue Heron, which is larger and has a longer neck and bill, fishes deeper in the water. Roseate Spoonbills and Wood Storks have uniquely shaped bills and are tactile feeders. They catch fish, crabs, crayfish, frogs, and insects that live in or near the muddy bottom. White Ibises, with their long, curved bills, take tactile feeding a step further and can even forage in grass and on muddy banks. Black-crowned and Yellow-crowned Night Herons fish after dusk when the other birds are resting. This habitat partitioning ensures that there is enough food for all the different birds.

GROWTH MINDSET

In the book, Jenny approaches the challenging task of learning how to fish with a Growth Mindset. Jenny views failure as a springboard for growth and learning. She is not afraid to work hard, try new strategies, or get input from others. She does not give up despite obstacles. Ultimately, her Growth Mindset results in success! The Growth Mindset concept is detailed further in Carol Dweck's bestselling book, *Mindset: The New Psychology of Success*.

ABOUT THE AUTHOR

Susan Sachs Levine grew up in Cincinnati, Ohio, and started her career in marketing with Procter & Gamble. She then moved to Columbus where she became VP of Marketing and Environmental Affairs with SIG, an international packaging company. A wildlife enthusiast, Susan has traveled extensively to learn about the natural world, especially endangered species.

After the birth of her two children, Susan focused her energy on serving as enrichment specialist at her children's schools. It was in this role that she identified the need for picture books about major Ohio cities. Her first book, *Packard Takes Flight: A Bird's-Eye View of Columbus, Ohio*, has become a standard in fourth grade classrooms when they study Ohio history. *Harriett's Homecoming: A High-Flying Tour of Cincinnati, Ohio*, highlights all that is special about the Queen City. Both books are based on the true story of Peregrine Falcons that nest on the tall buildings downtown.

Susan now lives in Naples, Florida, where she is enchanted by the wildlife, particularly the birds. She is a Florida Master Naturalist and excited to share all that she has learned about Florida's wading birds with children through her new work, *Jenny's First Catch: An Adventure with Florida's Wading Birds*.

In all her books, Susan blends her interest in wildlife with her imaginative storytelling to entertain and teach young children, while being a great resource for teachers and parents.

susanlevinebooks.com